We Love Bathtime!

Ready-to-Read

Simon Spotlight

New York   London   Toronto   Sydney

Based on the television series *Rubbadubbers*™ created by HIT Entertainment PLC
as seen on Nick Jr.®

by Alison Inches
photos by HOT Animation

 SIMON SPOTLIGHT

An imprint of Simon & Schuster Children's Publishing Division
1230 Avenue of the Americas, New York, New York 10020

Manufactured in the United States of America
First Edition   10 9 8 7 6 5 4 3 2 1

Library of Congress Cataloging-in-Publication Data
Inches, Alison.
We love bathtime! / by Alison Inches.— 1st ed. p. cm. — (Ready-to-read)
"Based on the television series Rubbadubbers as seen on Nick Jr."—T.p. verso.
Summary: The Rubbadubbers bath toys spend the day playing and then
enjoy more fun at bathtime.
ISBN 0-689-86881-2
(1. Toys—Fiction. 2. Play—Fiction. 3. Baths—Fiction.) I. Rubbadubbers (Television program) II. Title. III. Series.
PZ7.I355 Wdf 2004
(E)—dc22
2003018652

It is bathtime!

I like to splash!

I like to splosh!

I like to brush!

I like to wash!

I like to swim!

I like to fly!

We like to get wet!

I like to stay dry!

I like to play games!

We all like to play games!

We all like to play games!

I like to play games!

We love bathtime!